Cowboy Jess Saddles Up

Geraldine McCaughrean was born in North London. Her degree was in Education and she has been writing full time for many years, both adult and children's books. She has won the Whitbread Award, the Guardian Children's Fiction Award and the Beefeater Children's Book Award and has written several books for Orion, including *Myths and Legends of the World: The Golden Hoard*, *The Silver Treasure* and *The Bronze Cauldron*, *Stories from Shakespeare*, *God's People* and *Cowboy Jess*. She lives in Berkshire with her husband John and daughter Ailsa.

America

Cowboy Jess
Saddles Up

Geraldine McCaughrean

A Dolphin Paperback

For Matthew and Daniel

First published in Great Britain in 1996
by Orion Children's Books
a division of the Orion Publishing Group Ltd
Orion House
5 Upper St Martin's Lane
London WC2H 9EA
Dolphin paperback 1998

Typeset by Deltatype Ltd, Ellesmere Port, Cheshire
Printed in Great Britain
by Clays Ltd, St Ives plc

ISBN 1 85881 186 4

Contents

1

A Place to Call Home

A cowboy's bunk is special. During a hard day roping cattle, he thinks about it often – that warm, soft place where he can stretch out and sleep a well-earned sleep. But for Cowboy Jess Ford, his corner of the bunkhouse on the Lazy J Ranch, Paradise County, was even more special. It was the place where he belonged, a place to call home.

Found as a baby on the road west, between the wheel tracks of a wagon, curled up in a raccoon hat, the orphan Jess had been raised in a half-dozen places in and around Sundown Town. The people there looked on him with that kind of fondness they feel for a tree outside their gate, or a stray kitten.

But Jess wanted more. He wanted a place on the planet that he had earned for himself. The day good luck and cool nerves won him his wild black mare, Destiny, he proved he was ready for man's work. And the boss at the Lazy J had been prepared to take a chance on Jess – give him a job – despite his youth. Now there was a hard old shelf in the Lazy J bunkhouse which had a raccoon hat hung up over it; and carved in the timber wall alongside were the words *Jess Ford, Cowboy*.

The Widow Bramley had sewn him a quilt for his bed. But she did not pat him on the head so often – not now he was doing man's work.

Though Belle at the Silver Dollar Saloon had given him theatre and circus posters to brighten up the wall over his bed, she did not chuck him under the chin too often nowadays, or call him Jessie – not now he was a real working cowboy.

Of course some narrow-minded folk in town took against him when he made friends with 'that Sioux injun girl', Sweet Rain. She was half white, but that was not enough for them. They knew her heart rested entirely among the people of the buffalo, the hunting, restless, proud tribespeople whom Frontier settlers feared so much.

They made a team, Sweet Rain and Jess. Just like wild horses match each other, stride for stride, Jess and Sweet Rain went well together. They had more in common just than being motherless. She wove him a halter for his horse, from all the colours of the rainbow.

She also drew him a picture one day, trickling grains of coloured sand between her fingertips on to the ground, until she had created the shape of a black horse rearing, pawing the air, head among the clouds.

'Gee that's pretty!' he said. 'I wish I could take it home and pin it up over my bunk and see it every morning first thing, when I open my eyes.'

But Sweet Rain had only scraped her moccasin through the sand picture, blurring the pattern, breaking the image. 'Pictures should always be changing,' she said. 'If a tree is not bending and blowing, it's dead. If the view stays the same every day, your travelling must have ended. And your journey isn't over yet, Jess Ford.'

So now, when he woke, Jess Ford looked at the theatre posters on the wall, at the mascots and lucky horseshoes and handbills pinned up over the other men's bunks. And then he spent some time looking out of the window at the clouds moving, forming, colliding, reshaping themselves for ever and a day. After that he said to himself, 'Here's a new day for you, Cowboy Jess. Make the best of it.' And kicking off the quilt, he slid his feet into his boots.

2

Raising the Roof

Jess heaved the big Denver saddle off Destiny's back, and there it was – a nasty weal, livid like a blow from a whip. She flinched when he touched it.

He wanted to throw the heavy, misshapen saddle on the ground and kick it. But a cowboy is expected to look after his tack, and heaven help him if he doesn't. So Jess humped its huge weight into the tack room, the big stirrups banging his knees. He knew just how his poor horse felt; he had sore places very similar to Destiny, from sitting all day in that big ugly saddle.

All the cowboys on the Lazy J Ranch were issued with Denver saddles if they did not have a proper working saddle of their own. And a working saddle is a fancy piece of equipment, what with that big knob of a pommel at the front, strong enough to bring a roped steer to a standstill and all those extra straps for carrying a lariat, a shotgun, a branding iron . . . Even Denvers cost a mint of money, and as for the new Californians . . . well, Jess would never afford one.

He sighed and went to find a poultice for the saddle sore on his horse. Afterwards, all he wanted was to rest his own aching bones in the bunkhouse. And there, like an answer to a prayer, he saw the notice. It was pinned up over Jingle Bob's bunk.

BARN RAISING Joe Rafferty's place, Saturday. Cookout. Music. Dancing.
Giant Horseshoe Pitching Contest: Prize, one Saddle.

Jess went straight to the stable yard to root about for cast horseshoes. By the time he had walked the paddock and the breaking coral, he had collected an armful of shoes to practise with.

Once Jess Ford took an idea into his head, there was no shaking it loose. He made up his mind to get so good at pitching horseshoes that no one since the game was invented would beat him at it. So he practised, morning and evening, and even carried a few horseshoes with him out to his day's work (which weighed even heavier on Destiny's sore back).

Whenever one of the small-time ranchers, like Joe Rafferty, had a barn to build, he would throw a barn dance. Then, all his neighbours would come around and help him haul the huge walls and the panels of the roof into place – a job needing forty good strong men. In return the rancher's wife would feed them and their families, and the rancher would buy in a band and a barrel of beer. The dancing could go on so long everyone forgot they'd done any work at all raising the barn. It was about the best fun simple, honest folk could hope for.

But Jess was after that prize of a saddle. So he practised throwing horseshoes at a metal tent peg, until the other cowhands threw similar things at him. '*Quit that clang, clang, clanging, will you, boy!*' He got so good that he could sling three shoes and have them spin – clang, clang, clang – round the tent peg, just like that.

On the day of the barn raising there were

7

more buggies and flatcarts parked at Joe Rafferty's place than stagecoaches at a Wells Fargo depot. Women arrived with cakes wrapped in muslin, and daughters wrapped in their first gingham dancing dresses. Cowboys arrived in boots too new for dancing, and headed straight for the beer. Small boys fell over the pulling ropes and climbed on the flat barn walls and got shouted at for splitting the planks. And Joe Rafferty and his wife went the rounds, he giving out hammers, she with a hatful of nails for each man to fill his pockets from.

Jess made for the pitching range. There hung the prize saddle, propped on a trestle for all to see. It was a Denver.

Jess swallowed his disappointment. 'Don't know what put it in my head it would be a Californian,' he told his horse. Even so it was a beauty, what with the dark leather tooling, the shiny stirrups, the thick gleaming panniers.

'All hands to the ropes!'

Menfolk from Sundown and from all over Paradise County ranged themselves round the barn. Joe Rafferty gave the signal.

'Heave!' shouted the wives and children.

'Heave!' shouted the old men and the band.

'Heave!' shouted Joe Rafferty louder than anyone.

At first it seemed as if the walls were glued to the ground, but once the air got under them, they shucked free with a flurry of dust, and rose like the sails of a ship to the masthead. Ladders went up. Men ran up the ladders and began hammering, their mouths full of nails, their faces screwed up against the noise. Then the walls were declared secure, and the roof panels went up, like Roman legionnaires storming a castle under cover of their shields.

The grunts and panting gave way to sighs of satisfaction at a job well done. Joe Rafferty gave his wife a hug. It is every rancher's finest hour, the day his barn goes up. 'Just leaves the weathervane!' said Joe. His plump little wife tugged his sleeve and whispered in his ear, so that he looked around for Jess. 'Jess Ford!'

In Sundown they gave Jess jobs like that. Being an orphan from nowhere, brought up here and there by everyone and no one, he was like a town mascot. The superstitious reckoned he was lucky – look at that fine horse of his – and the sentimental reckoned he was the nicest kid in town. So when it came to weathervanes, and cutting first turfs and planting rose bushes, Jess often found himself in demand. 'Jess Ford!'

They loaded on to his back the big black iron casting of a running horse, and sent him up the ladder. He edged his way along, straddling the roof ridge, until the people below shouted, 'There! There!' Then he fixed the brackets in place with a mouthful of nails. Solid as a rock.

'Looks just like you, Destiny,' thought Jess, admiring the shining black silhouette of the metal horse. And he looked round for a sight of his own horse, far below, making a mental promise: I'll win you that saddle, girl. I will.

That was when the wind blew. A great gust which made the barbecue flare up, filled the girls' skirts and banged the new barn doors. The cast-iron weathervane swung round, and its black metal hooves caught Jess such a crack on the head that they knocked him clean off the roof ridge.

He slithered head-first down the steep slope, watching his hat spin out into space, hearing his boot toecaps rattle down the roof. There wasn't even a gutter to save him!

So he made a grab for the only thing that

would – a long nail that had gone in crooked and not banging home. It tore into the palm of his hand, but it stopped him plummeting over the edge to his death in the yard below. His feet overtook his head and dangled out over the upturned, open-mouthed faces watching. For a moment, everyone held their breath, nobody moved.

Then someone shouted, 'The haycart!' and the rest ran to pull the cart over close against the barn, so that Jess could drop down on to the soft bales of hay. 'You all right, boy? You fit?'

They thought for a while that the weather-vane had knocked all the wits out of him: Jess just sat on the hay and looked into his lap. But it was not the blow to his head that had done the damage. His right hand – the one he used to throw horseshoes – was cut to the bone and already bruised to the colour of plums. 'How am I going to pitch with that?' he murmured repeatedly, as Mrs Rafferty bandaged it tenderly.

Then, when the horseshoes were brought out, they were the big kind, from ploughing horses with feet the size of elephants'. Jess could barely lift one with his left hand, let alone throw it. He tossed one.

	'Wide!'
He tossed another.	'Bad luck!'
He tossed a third.	'Touch, no ringer!'

And he was out of the competition.

That gusting wind brought a shower of rain racing in from the north. It did not dampen spirits, though, for the barn-dancers just piled into the barn, moving the hay indoors with them, bale by bale, out of the wet. Women and children all lent a hand. Never again would the barn stand empty of this wispy gold, the farmer's livelihood, his guarantee against winter starvation for his animals. But today it was merely seating for the old folk, while the youngsters began the dancing, on the clear, central area, with a spirited Redowa – everyone's favourite dance.

Joe Rafferty made a speech thanking everyone for their help, and the minister read some piece out of the Bible about Joseph building barns in Egypt. The doctor recited *Paul Revere's Ride*, which was not exactly relevant but was very exciting. There was beef and mutton, bread and cheese, and the band — a dulcimer, squeezebox, flute and violin — made the sweetest music anyone ever danced to on a full stomach, while a gnarled old-timer sang:

Where is the girl who will go out west with me?
We'll live in some desired place, and happy we will be.
We'll have a little cabin with the ground for a floor,
A distance for a window and a plank for a door. So —
Will you go out west, will you go out west?
  will you go out west with me?
Will you go out west, will you go out west?
  Oh say, will you go out west with me?

When enough of the food had been danced off, the suggestion was made — as it always was — of a tug-of-war using a rope from the barn raising. The rain had stopped, but nails and planks and puddles were still strewn about the farmyard, so the teams trailed farther and farther away in search of a good flat site — no unfair lumps or slopes or rabbit-holes. The most extraordinary people joined in. Musicians, housewives, and dancing girls from the Silver Dollar Saloon squeezed in between the big brawny cattlehands. Little children lashed about

13

on the rope's ends like the papers on a kite string.

Not Jess, of course. His hand, bandaged big as a pumpkin, made him useless to either team, and so he took himself off to the paddock to apologise to his horse.

'I really messed up, Destiny,' he said. 'I surely and truly messed up.' The mare nuzzled him and sniffed at his hurt fist. 'Time to put this bent old saddle on and go home, lady,' he said, lifting the tack as gently as possible on to her sore back. But as he fastened the girth, Destiny suddenly threw up her head – almost like the weathervane swinging round. Her nostrils flared, her eyes rolled, and she gave that snorting hinny Jess had learned to recognise as a warning. Looking back at the barn, he saw an ominous orange glimmer.

Wisps of straw fallen from each bale as it was carried into the barn had made a yellow pathway across the yard. Some had blown across the barbecue, then dropped burning to the ground, igniting others. A wriggling snake of bright flame was even now creeping in at the door of the barn.

One hand in Destiny's mane, and Jess was

astride her. She did not hesitate, but leapt into a gallop, even though he as riding her directly towards fire, orange fire! The tug-of-war was happening on the far side, down towards the river; there was no time to fetch help. Jess slid down from the horse and began to stamp on the burning straw.

For a few short moments he thought he had it licked. But the flame just leapt ahead of his boots and straight into the heart of the hay bale where the band had been sitting. He slung the dulcimer out of the door, pocketed the flute, tucked the violin under his arm and stuck his wrist through the squeezebox handle. When the bale flared up, and Jess jumped backwards he made a noise like a one-man band. There was a sweet smell of laurel burning where Mrs Rafferty had tacked up pretty evergreen gorlands.

Jess knew he had to pull that burning bale away from the others or the whole barn would be gone in minutes.

But he had no sooner moved it a yard than the bandage round his hand caught light. With a roar of panic he fled outside and plunged the blazing gauze into the horse trough. Destiny stood there on her hind feet, pawing her front hooves at the detestable enemy: fire. Jess carried a couple of handfuls of water to the barn, but it was hopeless, and he knew it.

So, picking up another length of rope, he sank it in the trough to dampen it, then lashed one end round the pommel of his saddle.

'We have to go in there, Des!' he told the horse. 'Do you think you can do it?'

Ride a horse into a burning building? No man there that day would have believed it was possible. Fire strikes such paralysing terror into a beast that it is all a horse can do to move at the sight of it. But Destiny went into that barn because she trusted Jess to bring her out again. They galloped in through the low door as into an oven full of choking black smoke. They circled the burning bale and rode blindly back out again, so that the damp rope was looped around a half-hundredweight of blazing straw. Jess secured the other rope-end to the pommel, and Destiny towed the hay at her heels like a fiery golden chariot.

As they cleared the doorway, Jess was dimly aware of a bell clanging tunelessly in his head.

Someone else had seen the fire and was raising the alarm.

Mrs Rafferty said, 'I knowed he was good luck! Didn't I say, Joe? Jess Ford would bring our barn good luck?'

Jess smiled ruefully and drank another glass of fruit punch, hoping it would dull the pain.

'I don't believe Mister Ford thinks that our barn has brought *him* much luck, my dear,' said Joe. 'First his hand, now his saddle.'

'My saddle?' said Jess. He could not recall telling Joe Rafferty about his disappointment over the horseshoe pitching.

'Yeah. Ain't you seen it? Tail-strap's busted and one of the stirrup leathers is burned clean through. We'll have to fix you up with a new one.'

'Well make it a good one,' said his wife. 'Without Jess we'd've lost our barn the same day that we raised it!'

There was a ripple of applause from all the muddy, smoke-grimed party-goers who had run back from the tug-of-war to trample and douse the last glimmers of fire. Jess blushed.

'Oh, only the best for Cowboy Jess,' agreed

Joe. 'Reckon that Californian of mine is the fanciest I can lay hands on. Won it at the stock fair. But I reckon I'm too old to get used to this new-fangled tack.'

It weighed as light as a thirty-pound feather, and when Jess mounted up, his legs were in direct contact with Destiny's flanks instead of wedged outwards by huge flaps of leather. The skirt was tooled with swags of flowers, and there were silver eyelets with dangling fronds of leather – for no good reason but that they looked pretty. On the way home Destiny, free of the cumbersome weight of the old twisted saddle, sprang along, lifting her hooves high. And Jess, feeling her muscles ripple beneath the curve of his thigh, felt like a centaur, half-man, half-horse, halfway to being immortal.

3

The Medicine Bag

'I had to talk to somebody,' said Sweet Rain. 'I'm afraid.'

That was unusual enough: his friend Sweet Rain never admitted to being afraid. Jess was still more astonished by what she was carrying. Strapped to her back was a kind of rigid, box-shaped pouch, and peeping out of it was a baby about one year old.

'Oh, he's not *mine*,' said Sweet Rain, seeing Jess's face. 'He's the Chief's son. I'm looking after him for the Chief. His wife is ill.'

Was that why she was afraid? Was the lady someone dear to her, maybe? 'I am sorry,' he said.

'Oh, it's all part of the bad medicine. Because of the bag. His medicine bag. It's been stolen.' She looked at Jess to see if he understood the full dreadfulness of what she had told him, then wrinkled her nose in disgust. 'You don't understand anything, you white eyes.'

Jess shuffled his feet. They were standing outside the church-house in the middle of Sundown on a Sunday evening, and already Jess was attracting some very odd looks by talking to a Sioux girl with a baby. If Sweet Rain erupted into one of her rages, she was likely to get them both thrown in jail for disturbing the Sunday peace. 'You just explain it to me, then.'

Well, it seemed there had been a pow-pow on Sioux land: Major Bull from Paradise Fort, a Dakota Sioux chief called Punching Hare, and Chief Golden Eagle of the Lakotas. They had met to discuss the recruitment of Indian scouts into the army. The meeting had passed off fine, but when Golden Eagle had scraped his pipe and the visitors got up and gone, the Chief's medicine bag was gone, too. 'He thinks Punching Hare must have taken it! Now he's talking about going on the warpath – going to war, Jess! I've never seen a war inside a tribe!'

All the while she spoke, Sweet Rain was caressing something like a dead stuffed animal which hung from her belt. He asked to see it.

The hand which entrusted it to him was trembling.

'This is *your* medicine bag, is it?' he asked gently. It was a mole, black and glossy, its mouth agape, its little stomach as round as when it was alive. 'What's inside?'

'Only dry grass,' she said. 'And luck. And my prayers. Chief Golden Eagle's medicine bag is a fox – a beautiful fox. This long. Since he lost it, his wife has got sick, his horse has gone lame . . . He's afraid the baby will die if he stays near so much bad medicine. That's why I've been sent away with him.'

Coincidence, Jess wanted to say. Silly superstition. But he knew that his eyes were blue, and that made him see the world a whole different way from brown-eyed Sweet Rain, the Sioux. 'I'll tell you what we do,' said Jess. 'First thing tomorrow, we go and tell Major Bull up at the Fort. He needs to know if there's trouble brewing among the Sioux. Maybe he can cool things down. Maybe he remembers something about the medicine bag.'

'Maybe he stole it himself,' growled Sweet Rain. 'To make war between the tribes.'

'He's not that wicked,' said Jess feelingly.

'And he's not that clever. He would never dream a war could start up over a dead fox.'

Sweet Rain looked sideways at him, to see if he was disparaging the beliefs of her people. But Jess was busy playing with the baby, pulling his mouth out sideways and sticking his tongue in and out.

'He's bonny. What's his name?'

'A name has not shown itself yet to the shaman – the man of magic. It is not decided.'

Jess could not cope with that. Medicine bags, yes, but a baby with no name. He had been a baby without a name himself, until the people of Sundown had adopted him, and he knew what a gift they had given him the day they named him. A person can't get by without a name. 'Well, I'll call you Harry, then, till they give you something better,' he told the baby, and the baby laughed right out, just like that.

Major Bull was quick to grasp the seriousness of the situation. 'You did right to tell me, Sweet Rain, Jess. How long do you think we have?'

'My Chief says he will wait two days for the thief to come to his senses,' said Sweet Rain.

'My guess is,' said Jess shrewdly, 'he's waiting for his horse to get fit. It's lame right now.'

Major Bull gnawed his lip. 'Two days to stop a war, eh? I'd best ride over to the Dakotas and see if I can find out the truth. I don't see it, myself. It's not like Punching Hare to steal from his kin. Anyway, I saw that there fox hanging up in the tipi. I *saw* it, and it wasn't anywhere near Punching Hare. To get it, he'da had to step clean over Sergeant Gumper . . . Fine baby, that. What's his name?'

'Harry,' said Jess before Sweet Rain could answer.

'Where are we going?' asked Sweet Rain as they crossed the parade ground towards the barracks. The soldier on sentry duty wanted to know the same thing.

'Looking for Sergeant Gumper, sir,' said Jess straightening to attention almost. 'Message from Major –'

'Well, you won't find him in there,' said the sentry. 'He's off duty, lucky devil. Gone to town.'

So Jess and Sweet Rain headed for the gate.

'You think this Gumper has the medicine bag?' said Sweet Rain.

'I think there's a good chance of it,' said Jess. 'Gumper was sitting closest to it. Also, he has a liking for pretty ladies, and pretty ladies are kinda fond of fox fur. It makes a real fashionable neck-warmer.'

'Golden Eagle's medicine bag!' exclaimed Sweet Rain aghast. 'Used for a – a –'

'Doesn't bear thinking about, does it? So let's find him while he still has it on him – *if* he has it at all, that is.'

They mounted up, he on his black mare, she on her pinto. And they dug in their heels to ride. But of course the baby on Sweet Rain's back was quickly tossed about like a pea in a rattle. There was a padded hoop round his head, with charms and toys hanging down from it. But even with their cushioning softness, the exquisite cradle boards of the Sioux are not designed for a high-speed gallop. Sweet Rain had to rein in. 'You go ahead, Jess,' she said. 'If you're right, you could stop a war.'

Jess raised his hand in farewell, as he spurred Destiny on towards Sundown Town.

He found Sergeant Gumper at the barber's

shop, having a shave and a haircut. But delight at finding him dwindled, as Jess wondered what to do next. He could hardly walk straight up and ask, 'Did you steal a medicine bag from Chief Golden Eagle during the pow-wow?' Gumper might be small and balding and wear the buttons of his jacket undone to make room for his belly; but he had big fists. Anyway, he was not likely to admit to such a thing and say goodbye to his job in the army.

He had a big cloth bag at his feet. 'It's in there,' thought Jess, and promptly dropped a handful of coins on the floor, accidentally on purpose. Pretending to look for the money, he crawled his way over to the bag.

'Hey, what'ya doing, kid?' The sergeant lashed out with his boot. 'Get off my bag!'

'Dropped my money,' said Jess apologetically, and retreated. There had been nothing in the bag. He climbed up into the chair beside Gumper.

'Be with you in two shakes, Jess,' said the barber, 'though you won't be needing a shave for a while yet, I'll wager! Ha ha ha!'

'Got to look good if I'm gonna get myself a girl,' said Jess brashly. The barber's eyebrows shot up. He had never heard Jess Ford talk like that before. Sergeant Gumper gave a snort of disdain. Jess went on: 'How d'ya do it, Sergeant Gumper? You're real popular with the ladies, aren't you?'

That startled him. He coloured up with pleasure. 'I've broken a few hearts, sure,' he admitted proudly.

'Who's the lucky lady this week?' said Jess. He could see the barber scowling at him for being a coarse, rude boy.

'Reckon you could say Belle at the Silver Dollar Saloon is pretty glad to see me these days,' boasted the fat little man, admiring himself in the mirror. That was the information Jess was after.

The barber flicked his towel, and Gumper's shave was finished. Jess was just about to dash out of the shop when – flick – he found the towel round his own neck, and the barber began to comb roughly at his unruly hair. 'How short you want it, *Mister* Ford?'

'I got to go!'

'Nonsense. I thought you wanted to impress the girls. Or were you just talking big, by any chance? Sit still and I'll soon have you tidied up.' And he began to snip.

'No! No!' yelled Jess. 'I just remembered! The girls I know like long hair!' and he wriggled out of the seat and fled. At the door he turned and apologised: 'I'll explain some other time. It's a matter of life and death, you see!'

Down at the Silver Dollar, Belle was on stage singing. Jess would have to wait patiently until she had finished. One song. Two songs. Saints alive! he thought. She's going to sing for ever! Then, as she came down from the stage, cowboys and soldiers and businessmen all converged on her, offering to buy her a drink. Belle was a real popular girl.

'She's with me!' said Jess, dodging between them and taking Belle's arm. 'Bartender, bring us some . . . something or other.'

Fortunately Belle had a soft spot for Jess. Her ma had looked after him for a while when he was a baby, sleeping him in a purple and white striped hat box behind the stage. 'What's got into you, Jess Ford?'

'Come and sit down and I'll tell you.'

The bartender squinnied at Jess, barber's towel still tucked round his neck, and brought two sarsaparillas, judging the boy could not afford anything stronger and was too young to drink it anyway. 'Did Sergeant Gumper give you a medi – a fox fur?'

'Well, fancy you knowing! He did, yes. Not two hours back.'

'Can I have it? I must have it! *Please*! It was stolen.'

Belle narrowed her eyes in a way that made her round, flat little face look like a cougar's. 'Typical! Stolen goods. Ain't that just typical of that little show-off Gumper!' She patted Jess on the head maternally. 'I would help, I surely would . . . but I can't, little pal,' she said. 'I figured if Jake – that's my *real* sweetheart – if Jake saw me with a fox fur given me by some other beau, then that other beau might get his jaw broke. Terrible temper, my Jake.'

'Not as terrible as Golden Eagle,' said Jess under his breath. 'So where is the bag . . . fox-fur now, Belle?'

'I gave it to Cynthia. One of the other girls.'

'And where's Cynthia?'

'Gone home poorly. Funny. It came on her all of a sudden.'

'Where does she live?'

28

'Well, I *could* tell you, but . . .'

'Please, Belle! It's a matter of life and death!'

'. . . but before she went home, she sent the fox fur up the street – told old Posie Mayflower to work it up into a hat.'

'*A hat!?*'

Sarsaparilla spilled all over the table, all over Jess's hat, all over Belle's dress. Jess got up and ran, chased out of the saloon by shouts and jeers.

Sweet Rain was just trotting into town, singing to the baby on her back. Jess ran wildly past her, shouting something about a hat and a haberdashery. She followed him as fast as she was able, hampered by the cradle board.

Posie Mayflower was a pinch-mouthed old lady who thought God had made America for the sole use of spinsters and shopkeepers. She took one look at Sweet Rain and began to fan herself with a swatch of cloth samples. In the other hand she held a huge pair of scissors. And curled up in front of her on the counter, for all the world like a living animal, was a foxskin lightly stuffed, its brush an orange flame tipped with white.

'No injuns in here!' barked Miss Mayflower.

'Git!' Sweet Rain retreated, accustomed to such unkindness.

'That fox –' said Jess, breathless from running.

'What about it?'

'Did Cynthia send it?'

'Yep. To be made into a hat. Not that it's any business of –'

'*You can't.*'

'I beg your pardon, young man?' Miss Mayflower was as tall as a beanpole and twice as whippy. She brandished her scissors.

'You mustn't, Miss Maypole – I mean Miss Mayflower. I mean . . . it's a matter of –'

Jess stopped. He knew that Posie Mayflower had no time for 'injuns'. If he told her what the medicine bag really was, she would probably slash into it then and there, in front of his very eyes, calling it a pagan, demon-worshipper's toy. She would be positively glad to start a war among the tribes.

'Rabies!' said Jess so loud that Miss Mayflower jumped. 'The fox had rabies! Could infect anyone who wears it! Foaming at the mouth! Biting people! Horrible!'

'*Blaagch!*' cried Posie Mayflower, dropping

her scissors. 'Get it out of here! Pleeeease, young man! *Get it out!*'

Jess obliged.

Outside on the boardwalk, he laid the medicine bag in Sweet Rain's open arms. 'Is there still time?' he asked.

'If I ride like the wind,' said Sweet Rain. She looked round distractedly at the baby in its cradle board. She could not gallop with him on her back!

'Then you'd best give me Harry to look after. I'll fetch him along at an easy walk,' Jess promised. 'First I'd better clean and vittle him. I suggest you don't tell Golden Eagle what happened to his bag. Just say we looked and we found it, okay?'

As Sweet Rain's pinto thundered out of town, Jess turned back towards the Silver Dollar Saloon for a well-earned drink. 'Two glasses of milk, please, bartender,' he said with a grin, 'and some place quiet, where I can clean up Harry.'

By the time Jess delivered Harry back to Chief Golden Eagle, his wife, his horse and his good nature had all recovered. He put it down to the return of his medicine bag, of course, and for that he thanked Jess and Sweet Rain.

'Any time,' said Jess with a shrug. 'I carved something for Harr – for the little one,' and he pulled out a small wooden horse he had carved with his whittling knife.

The shaman – a fearful-looking man hung about with all manner of dead animals and snakes – lurched forward and grabbed the carving. He shouted something so loud that everyone in the tipi flinched.

'He says the baby's name has come,' Sweet Rain translated. 'He says the baby must be called Medicine Horse.'

'*Harry* Medicine Horse,' said Golden Eagle, smiling a rare smile. (Sweet Rain must have told him what Jess had called the baby, and he rather liked it.)

'Harry Medicine Horse,' said Jess delightedly, and the baby laughed out loud – just like that – which Sweet Rain told him later was the best possible omen.

4

Posse

Smith was big. That was the first thing people noticed about the blacksmith at the Sundown livery stables. He was BIG. He could swing a hammer like other men swing a walking cane, and bend horseshoes without heating them. People said if a horse wouldn't pick its feet up to be shod, Smith would pick up the whole horse and shoe it that way.

Anyway, whenever Sheriff Sparrow needed to raise a posse of deputies, the first man he thought of was Ned Smith.

One morning, the Pony Express rider crawled into Coney Creek saying he'd been robbed. The whole county was alerted to look out for the bandit – a big, dangerous type last seen heading down the trail towards Sundown.

When Sheriff Sparrow heard the news he frowned. He would have to get together a posse

– swear in half-a-dozen men as deputies – and go looking for this bandit. That wasn't going to be easy. Half the town was away visiting the State Fair and he'd just burned both hands taking a skillet off the stove. 'What kind of a sheriff goes around bandaged up like an Egyptian mummy?' he thought glumly looking at his injured hands. Ah well. He could make a start by swearing in Big Ned Smith. Ned was worth three pairs of hands.

The Sheriff strolled along to the livery stables. All the way down the street he could hear Smith hammering away in the forge. 'Hey, Ned!' he called, but the blacksmith did not reply. Not surprising. Being around that kind of noise all day, Ned Smith was getting pretty deaf. Sparrow watched the man plunge a red-hot horseshoe into the water bucket; it made a hiss like forty locomotive trains letting off steam. While the Sheriff waited patiently for the din to die down, he looked all around.

That was when he saw them: four Pony Express saddle bags, large as life, slung over the roof beam.

The stolen bags? In Ned Smith's forge? Sparrow backed slowly out of the forge and, when he reached the sunlit door, turned and made a run for it.

Ned Smith! Of course! Hadn't the Pony Express rider described the bandit as 'big and dangerous'?

'Someone call?' said Ned Smith laying aside his big hammer and tongs. But when he looked around, there was no-one to be seen.

The Sheriff went straight to Dr Luke's. 'Jumping snakes, Luke, hurry and let me in, cain't you?'

The Doctor opened his door. 'G'day Sheriff. How are those hands of yours today? Come for a fresh bandage? You'll have to wait your turn, I'm afraid. It's a busy day.'

'Dang it, Luke, I need a posse, not a bandage!' Sheriff Sparrow looked around him wildly. Of the patients in the surgery, three were old ladies, one was a woman expecting a baby, one was Moses Froggett and the last was a ranch hand with his arm in a a sling.

'Raise your right hand, cowboy!' said the Sheriff.

'Would if I could,' said the cowboy with a rueful grin, 'But it's broke in three places.'

Moses Froggett raised a trembling right hand lined and leathery with seventy years of hard toil. 'I'll volunteer, Sheriff,' he croaked.

Doctor Luke had other ideas. 'Moses is eighty-three years old, Sheriff. You can't swear him in. I won't allow it.'

'Then you'll have to come yourself!' said Sheriff Sparrow growing quite red in the face. 'Ned Smith has robbed the Pony Express in Coney Creek and I have to arrest him!'

'Ned Smith?' exclaimed everyone in the room.

'I seen the proof with my own eyes. Now raise your right hand, young man, or I'll throw you in jail for obstructing the Law!'

'Very well,' said Doctor Luke unwillingly. 'But you know I don't own a gun – don't hold with firearms. I won't carry one, even for you.'

Sheriff Sparrow gave a snort of frustration and led the way down the road to the Silver Dollar Saloon. There were always plenty of strong young men to be found drinking in there.

The swing doors were tied shut with a piece of string and on the string hung a notice: CLOSED FOR THE FAIR. The Sheriff kicked the wall. 'Where am I gonna find a posse of men to tackle Big Ned Smith? He could tie knots in a bull's horns with his bare hands! I need manpower!'

Just then, Herbert the bank-teller came out of the bank with Minnie Good on his arm. Sheriff Sparrow immediately swore him in as a deputy. Herbert did not mind at all: he liked the starry look in Minnie's eyes as he became 'an official deputy law enforcer for the US Government' and pinned on the metal star. With a smarmy smile and a swagger of the hips, he whipped out his shiny silver pistol and used it to tip his hat back on his head. Minnie giggled with delight. 'Who are we after, Sheriff?' he asked in a cool drawl.

'Ned Smith,' said Sparrow. 'Robbed the Pony Express out near Coney Creek.'

Herbert dropped his gun with a clatter on the boardwalk. 'Big Ned did? Honest?'

Cowboy Jess was in town buying supplies for the Lazy J bunkhouse. Seeing the excitement outside the saloon, he went over.

'Raise your right hand!' said the Sheriff.

'Who, me?'

'Every man has to do his duty when his country asks it,' said Sheriff Sparrow.

'Isn't he a bit young?' asked the Doctor.

'Oh, that's okay,' said Jess cheerfully, and his chest swelled with pride as the Sheriff tossed him a deputy's nickel star. 'It's just that I don't have a gun yet, sir.'

Sheriff Sparrow gave a whinny like a horse and stomped off muttering and cussing, followed by his motley little posse: the Sheriff was having a very bad day.

Mr Mayflower the grocer was out fishing, but Posie Mayflower, his sister said she would come along. The Sheriff thanked her and said that wouldn't be necessary, but she came anyway, because she was the town busy-body and wanted to see what was going on.

At the funeral parlour they swore in the undertaker in his tall black hat and flapping black cloak. He picked up a large-bore shotgun from its rack, and was halfway out of the door when he remembered it was not loaded. Turning back, he said, 'I'll just get some ammunit- OW!' That was just the moment Sheriff Sparrow chose, in a fever of impatience, to slam the shop door shut – right on the undertaker's hand.

'I'm sorry! I'm sorry! I'm a gosh-darned, solid gold-plated, ham-fisted idiot! I never saw you!' howled the Sheriff, as Doctor Luke examined the poor man's broken trigger finger. 'What's happening in this town today? There's Big Ned Smith turned to lawlessness, and the rest either gone away or unfit for duty! How am I gonna overpower a man like Ned Smith with a posse like this – one man-of-peace, a kid, a woman and a bunch of winged ducks!'

'You could always . . .' Jess began to say, but Herbert interrupted.

'Don't forget me! I'm real handy with a gun.'

'You could ride out to the ranches and round up a few cowboys,' suggested Posie Mayflower.

But the Sheriff said there was no time. 'It's no good. We just gotta go in there armed to the teeth and somehow make him come quietly.' Sparrow gave a weary sigh. 'Truth is, I like the man. I don't want him putting up a fight and getting hurt in the struggle.'

'Not much chance of that,' muttered the Doctor under his breath, but everyone knew how the Sheriff felt. Everyone liked Big Smith.

'We could always just . . .' Jess began, but the Sheriff called for silence.

Clang clang clang, the noise of Smith's hammer clamoured down the street. The little posse stood around the public horse trough, undecided what to do next. Herbert pulled out his gun and began twirling it. It flew off his finger end and fell with a splash into the horse trough.

Sheriff Sparrow said he was the sorriest apology for a deputy ever to get out of bed, and Posie Mayflower said his brains were good for nothing but to make india rubbers. 'Now what?' said the Sheriff despairingly.

'I've got an idea,' said Jess. 'You stay here.' And before anyone could stop him, he had unhitched his horse, who was drinking from the trough, and led her over to the livery stables.

'Don't do anything reckless!' Doctor Luke called after him.

Big Smith looked twice as big as Jess remembered. The bulging muscles of his bare arms were plaited like ship's rope, and his face was black from the forge. Firelight glinted red in his eyes.

'Hi there, Mr Smith!' said Jess. 'Can you shoe Destiny for me, please?'

The blacksmith's face broke into a broad smile. 'Right away, son! Love the feel of a beautiful horse like yours between my hands. Kinda makes my day.' Armed with a huge pair of pincers, he moved round Destiny and, gentle as gentle, picked up each of her feet in turn. 'The front shoes aren't much worn, boy. They'll last you another month.'

'Okay. Just the back ones, then,' said Jess.

While the blacksmith worked, Jess looked up high and peered through the smoke from the forge.

Sure enough, just as the Sheriff had said, there were the tell-tale Pony Express saddle-bags, hanging down over the roofbeam.

'What are those Pony Express bags doing up there, Mr Smith?' asked Jess. Straight out, just like that.

Ned Smith looked up, his mouth so full of nails that it was a while before he could answer. 'Them? Oh, they belong to some guy staying over at the hotel. He liveried his horse here – that sorry looking nag in the end stall. Didn't much like the look of him: little pipsqueak of a fellah. Seemed to have trouble carrying them bags, so I slung them up there for him. Says he'll be back for them this afternoon . . . What's so funny? You gonna let me in on the joke? And what you doing wearing that deputy star, kid? You playing at lawman today?'

Jess glanced down at the badge on his shirt and, when he could stop laughing for long enough, unfastened it and held it out to the blacksmith. 'It's for you, actually. Sheriff Sparrow's rounding up a posse, and I reckon right now you're just the man he's looking for.'

So when Big Ned Smith came out of the forge – almost as broad as the door and as heavy as a wagon horse – he was wearing a deputy's star on his vest. He was rather startled to see the sheepish little crowd crouching down behind the horse trough opposite. Herbert the bank-teller had one sleeve rolled up to the shoulder and was groping about in the trough trying to find something.

At the sight of the blacksmith, they all turned as white as ghosts.

Jess called out very loudly, as he and Smith crossed the road: 'Mr Smith is quite happy to serve as a deputy, sir. And – good news! – he knows exactly where the bandit is holed up.'

'He does?!' said the posse in one voice.

'I do?' said the blacksmith, much surprised.

'Yes. The Pipsqueak with the saddlebags. At the hotel. Unfortunately, Sheriff Sparrow is a little . . . ah . . . short-handed at the moment.'

Big Ned Smith looked pityingly down at the posse – bandaged, embarrassed and woebegone. 'Don't you worry about a thing, Sheriff Sparrow, sir,' he said in his huge, booming voice. 'If that guy at the hotel is a bandit, I'll just go and fetch him out, and you can lock him up in your jail.' And off he went, still holding his club hammer.

'I knew all along it couldn't be him!' said Sheriff Sparrow, blushing deeply and standing up from behind the horse trough.

'Always such a friendly, hard-working man,' said Mr Graves.

'Gentle with animals,' said Doctor Luke.

'Such a neighbourly, god-fearing man,' said Posie Mayflower the grocer's sister.

'D'you think we ought to go and help him arrest that bandit?' said Herbert, finally fishing his gun out of the trough.

'I think he might just manage without us,' said Jess.

And five minutes later, the blacksmith was back. He was carrying a thin, round-shouldered little stranger under one arm like a roll of carpet. 'Here you are, Sheriff. He didn't put up a struggle.'

'Sensible man,' said Jess. 'I think the Pony Express rider exaggerated a bit when he reported the robbery. I'll go and fetch the loot, shall I?'

By mounting up on Destiny's back, Jess was just able to reach the Pony Express saddle bags and pull them down from the roof beam. 'Guess that's my last duty as a deputy, Destiny,' he said to his horse, sadly. 'It's back to being plain Cowboy Jess from tomorrow.'

The horse gave a long, snorting breath. She did not want to leave the sweet-smelling warmth of the livery stable without the carrot Big Ned always kept by for his four-legged customers.

Big Ned Smith was the only man in the world, beside Jess, who could lay a hand on Destiny and live. Maybe that's how Jess had known all along that the blacksmith was no bandit – had never robbed the Pony Express, or anyone else, in his entire life. Horses are a great judge of character, and Jess and Destiny always shared their feelings about people.

5

Wrangler Jess

'Roll 'em out!' yelled Bossman J, but his voice was drowned out by the noise of the herd. A hundred head of cattle can make quite a din when they sense a change coming. The trail boss raised his fist in the air, and the autumn drive moved off.

It was one of those moments when Jess Ford wished he had a mother to write home to. 'Ma! Just leaving on my first drive – nigh two hundred miles to Stetson City. I'm riding *wrangler*, Ma!'

Though Bossman J himself stayed home, almost every other hand was needed for the epic journey. Obadiah was riding point, up near the front, Woolly was swing, mid-way down the herd and Jingle Bobs was on the flank, whipping in the stragglers. They were feeling pretty pleased with themselves for avoiding the worst kind of work – riding drag, bringing up the rear. But Jess was wrangler!

In point of fact, wrangler is the humblest job of the lot. It goes to the youngest, greenest cowhand and puts him at everyone's beck and call, helping out, filling in, standing by. But Jess loved the sound of it on his tongue, the feel of it on his lips: Wrangler Jess! He thought it was the best job in the entire world. For he was in charge of the remuda – the little band of spare horses needed when the cowboys' mounts or the team pulling the chuck wagon grew too tired.

When the cowboys grew tired, there was no one to give them a rest. From dawn till dusk they hustled the herd, driving the stragglers and the renegades back into the torrent of moving beef. The herd must not move too fast, or they would run off their fat. They must not move too slow or they would be late for the meat auctions in Stetson City. So on they rode, hour after hour, day after day in the saddle, until Jess thought he would be shaped like a wishbone for the rest of his life, and a pulled wishbone at that.

The remuda was easy to control. Destiny did all the work. She had such authority that the horses obeyed her commands like she was royalty. A queen among horses, that was what Jess thought of his beautiful black mare.

And king among the cattle was Johnny Appleseed. An enormous, grizzled brown bull, Johnny Appleseed was the Lazy J 'leader', and had been now for six successive years. Decked out with a giant brass bell on a thick leather collar, he strolled ahead of the herd, his gigantic mottled horns shining like a crescent moon. Cattle can be silly, nervous critters, jumpy as fleas. The least little thing can spook them. But while they had Johnny Appleseed in sight, they were peaceful, content to follow where he led, soothed by the clang, clang of the brass bell. But Johnny was getting old. Everyone supposed this would be Johnny Appleseed's last drive.

That first night, when the men pitched camp and hauled their bedrolls down off the chuck wagon, Jess slouched down exhausted against its wheel. Then he stood right up again and climbed on top of the cart as fast as his legs would carry him. For coming towards him was Johnny Appleseed, horns blood red in the last rays of the sun, mouth drizzling.

'He's only after you for an apple!' said

Cookie. 'Johnny always comes round at the end of the day begging for titbits. Di'n you known that, boy? Now get on down here, and gather me some firewood. That's the wrangler's job. Gotta get you doing some work after a day' shirking!'

So Jess hauled his aching bones away to scavenge for firewood, while Cookie opened up the travelling kitchen. He had a kind of chest of drawers in the back of the wagon, and in each drawer a different commodity – sugar, flour, coffee beans, cutlery, bandages and needles.

The stars were bright that night, with a haze round the moon. The herd were quiet – never silent, but quiet enough for Jess to hear the tinkling of the river where they had just drunk their fill. As he washed the dust out of his ears, the music of a cowpoke's mouth organ came drifting through the night air as sweet as honey dripping from a spoon.

Ten days out, there was a storm. It did not rain, but thunder began to rumble round the sky like the planets were on the roll. The heat hammered a cowboy's hat down over his eyes.

49

'Wouldn't take much to spook them now,' said the trail boss, an Irishman with a chestnut filly as ginger-maned as he was. 'The Beans River is just over that rise. Let's get them spread out before they smell the water.'

If thirsty cattle scent water, the ones at the back get eager and speed up, fearful that the cows in front will get to drink before them. They speed up, and bump and barge, and valuable cows get their hides nicked by jostling horns. So Jess and the others helped spread the herd out, side by side, instead of nose-to-tail, and Johnny Appleseed set a nice, easy pace.

Somewhere up-river the rain *had* begun, because the Beans River was swollen dangerously high. The trail boss took one look and said, 'Cain't take them over that, or we might lose the weaklings. We'll camp this side and hope it shallows out by tomorrow.' Another bolt of thunder clattered round the sky. 'Where's that wrangler?'

'Here, sir!' said Jess.

'No firewood duty for you tonight, son. You get over with them cows and sing to 'em.'

'*Sing*, boss?'

'Sure! Sing! You never been on a drive

before? Cattle like a lullaby. It soothes them. And right now we want them as calm as ducks on a pond.'

So Jess went to stand watch over the nervy, anxious cows, as they drifted back from drinking at the riverbank. And according to orders, he sang:

As I was a-walking one morning for pleasure,
I spied a cow-puncher a-strolling along.
His hat was throwed back and his spurs were a jingling,
And as he approached he was singing this song:
*   Whoopee ti yi yo, Git along little dogies*
It's your misfortune and some of my own.
Whoopee ti yi yo, Git along little dogies,
You know that Wyoming will be your new home.

He took an apple from his pocket for Johnny Appleseed, but the old-timer did not seemed interested for once. He only rolled his eyes and flicked his ears and gave a loud, long bellow. It was an oddly desolate noise, like someone calling his last farewell from a great way off. But it fetched up the heads of the grazing cattle. Clang, clang, clang went the bell round Johnny Appleseed's neck as he trotted down to the water.

51

Down to the water and into it.

'No, Johnny! Not tonight! We don't want you to cross over tonight!' said Jess, splashing up to his knees. 'The river's too high!' But the great bull took no notice, and what could Jess do? Short of grabbing hold of the old fellow by the horns, there was no stopping him. No one stops a ton of beef on the hoof.

Jess did not want to raise his voice, for fear of spooking the other cattle. He dared not fire off a shotgun to fetch help. But he needed it. Great eels and fishes, he needed it! For the whole herd was starting after Johnny Appleseed, confident as ever that he would lead them safely over the river and onward. The other cowboys were all unsaddling, settling down to rest. But Johnny Appleseed had decided he knew better; he was going to lead the herd on over the swollen Beans River!

Jess ran back to where Destiny stood prancing with alarm on her hind feet. 'We gotta do something, Destiny!' he said. By this time the others must have realised the herd was on the move. Jess judged it better to stay with the herd.

Now Johnny Appleseed must have sensed

that his long life was coming to an end, and wanted to go out in glory. Because out he swam, head back, jaw stiff, pumping away with his short, stocky legs. He made it across – all the way – though the current leaned on him and the driftwood banged him about. But just as he pulled himself out of the river on the other side, his great heart busted and he sank down on his knees, as peaceful as can be, and laid his crescent horns in the mud.

Destiny was a powerful swimmer, but to carry a rider over that muddy torrent made the veins beat in her neck and her nostrils gape and her own heart thud like a drum. Overhead, the thunder changed from a rumble to a crash – like God slamming his barn doors. A fork of lightning prodded the Lazy J herd. Jess slid from the saddle and swam along in the lee of Destiny's big black bulk. They were swept downstream, but they made it, washed up and climbed ashore right beside the peaceful body of Johnny Appleseed. Jess pulled out his Bowie knife and cut off the big brass bell. Then he stood on the shore and he rang it – clang, clang, clang – for the sake of the cattle in the water.

'If they think their leader's gone, they'll panic

and drown,' he told his horse. 'Now they're in the river, we gotta help them make it over.' So he tolled the big old cow bell, and the terrified cattle in the Beans River swam, heads up, horns clashing, towards the sound of the leader who had never failed them.

Half the herd stayed behind on the bank, headed off by Woolly and Jingle and the rest. Half tried to cross the river. A couple of the weaklings did get swept away by the flood-water, but the rest made it across, thanks to Jess and that bell. They came past Jess like a living thunderstorm, stinking of wet hide. With luck, they would spread out and graze in the gathering darkness. Jess began to sing, to soothe them:

> *Oh give me a home where the buffalo roam,*
> *Where the deer and the antelope play;*
> *Where seldom is heard a discouraging word*
> *And the skies are not cloudy . . .*

But his voice was drowned out by a thunder-clap like the crack of Doom, and the whole sky split apart with sheet lightning bright as day.

The cattle thought it was the end of the world. They threw back their horns, showed the whites of their eyes and took off as if their tails were on fire.

Jess could see the trail boss struggling across the river to help, but if Jess waited for him to arrive the cattle might run themselves over a precipice or scatter over twenty miles of desert. He had to try and head them off. He had to try.

They kicked up behind them a dustcloud so thick that they disappeared from sight. Jess pulled his bandanna over his nose and mouth, to keep from breathing in the dirt, clamped his hat hard down over his face and leapt into Destiny's sodden, squelchy saddle. 'We have to turn them girl!' he said. 'We can't let them win this race!'

Past the tail-end stragglers they galloped, past the fat ones and the steers with knock-knees. The air was thick as porridge with the dirt they kicked up, and the noise they made was one continuous, demented bellow. Cattle in a stampede leave behind their brains, their sense, any natural-born instinct for their own preservation. They just run, and the running empties their heads of everything but the need to run and go on running.

'We don't ride drag, do we?' yelled Jess into

the din. 'We don't ride flank!' as Destiny
overtook the back of the herd. 'We don't ride
swing!' he yelled as they drew level with the
centre of the stampede. 'We don't ride point!'
he yelled as they reached the foam-mouthed,
mad-eyed leaders of the pack.

Jess knew that to turn the herd he must slice
straight across the path of the stampede. If
Destiny stumbled, the cattle would stampede
over him and his horse without even noticing.
Bushes and cacti were invisible to them, so too
would be a fallen rider. 'Keep your feet, lady!'
he shouted, and brought round her head.

Straight and sure as an arrow, Destiny sliced
across in front of the herd. But she was black,
and the daylight was almost gone. The cattle did
not even see her!

'Once more, lady, and quick as you like!'
yelled Jess. Back they veered, slewing so close in
front of the leading bull that Jess saw the
waterdrops on its horns.

The cattle flinched – and turned, all the one
way, as swallows turn, sharing a single thought.
The herd wheeled back on itself like a water-
course suddenly dammed which swirls into a
whirlpool. Confused and finding cattleflesh on

all sides, the beasts gave up their stampede which decayed into a mindless, circling turmoil – the 'mill'. Jess could never have held it, but by now the trail boss was on the far side of the lumbering, wheeling mass. Into Jess's ears dawned the clang, clang of a bell. He might have thought it was the ghost of Johnny Appleseed till he looked down and realised he was still shaking the big brass cowbell and had been all along. As well as singing:

Oh give me a home where the buffalo roam
And the skies are not cloudy all day!

'You did well, cowboy,' said the trail boss. 'You should never have let them git started, but in the circumstances you did okay. For a greenhorn. That's one fine horse you got there.'

They stood oozing river water and sweat – and now rainwater too, as the electric storm finally broke and pouring rain slushed the thunder and dowsed the lightning. 'I heard you back there. "Don't ride flank, don't ride point . . ." I s'pose that means you're after my job, does it? Out front, leading the way? Fancy yourself trail boss, do you?'

'No, sir!' exclaimed Jess. 'not a bit of it! I've got the best job already, sir!' and he tilted his hat to a rakish angle. 'I'm the *wrangler*!' he said with pride.

The trail boss laughed and clapped him on the shoulder. 'Then you'd best get back and round up your remuda, wrangler. There's horses scattered everywhere from here to Mexico.'

6

Line Camp

'Oh, it's a terrible place, that Number 5,' said Obadiah Thorn, blowing into his mittens. 'Line camp's bad any time, but Number 5?' and he sucked his teeth.

'You're only kidding me,' said Jess with a laugh. 'There's no such thing as ghosts.'

Obadiah sucked his teeth again. 'Oooh. That's what Snowy Montana said . . . before he spent a week at Number 5.'

'Why d'ya think they called him Snowy?' said Jingle Bobs.

'Hair went white overnight,' said Woolly, 'with the fear.'

Jess took no notice. He knew they were trying to scare him. He had never worked a line camp before, and they seemed to think that called for some teasing. At Number 3 they dropped off Woolly; he did not seem very keen to go.

Line camp consists of single log cabins spaced every eight miles round the borders of a ranch. In winter, when deep snow makes riding the boundaries slow and dangerous, the cowhands don't return to their bunkhouse each night, but camp out, one at each of these cabins. It's lonely work – chasing off neighbours' cattle, watching out for wolves, stopping steers from straying. They left Jingle Bobs at Number 4; he looked real small and vulnerable standing by the shack door.

'They say it's the ghost of a cowboy,' Obadiah persisted. 'Got snowed in. Died of starvation.'

'I brought a book to read,' Jess retaliated. 'I mean to make the most of the peace and quiet, away from your yattering.'

That stopped their teasing. They could not come to terms with a cowboy being able to read. It always struck them dumb with amazement. But when Jess saw Number 5 cabin his heart sank. It was no more than a broken-down shed with a sod roof and snowdrifts all around. It took him half an hour to dig out the front door and get it open. By the time, Obadiah was a distant speck moving away through the snow towards Number 6.

The only sound was the groaning of two fir trees hard up against the back wall. The trees were starting to push the cabin over; big gaps were opening between the logs, and Jess spent the rest of the day packing them with snow.

'Well, Destiny,' he said, digging out a snow-shelter for his horse. 'Here we are for three weeks. Shall I read you a bedtime story or will you read me one?' If he could, he would have taken Destiny indoors, just for the company.

It was hot work digging, but as soon as he stopped, he realised he ought to have lit the stove first off, and got the hut warm. Now the kindling was wet, and it was too dark to find more. Then – disaster! – he got the stove alight only to find the flue was blocked with snow, so the hut filled up with smoke. When he went out to clear the flue, the melted snow fell down it like a cowpat, and put the fire out. Then the flue came away in his hands, and he tripped and put his foot through the roof.

In the end, Jess had to eat cold beans, curl up in all the blankets and rugs he could find, and watch the stars and the falling snow, as white as each other, through the hole in the roof. No time to think about Obadiah's ghost. Too tired.

At first light, though, he woke to the sound of howling and scrabbling and something shoving at the door. The hairs on his head stood straight up. He tried to push his cold feet into his boots, but the leather soles had frozen solid to the floor, so that he fell over the first step he took. The noise at the door got shriller – a whining, haunting noise.

'Who's there?' said Jess, and his voice came out high. 'Go away!' If it were a ghost, it would walk clean through the door, surely? But somehow that thought was not a comfort. It sure wasn't Destiny trying to come through that door.

Destiny! Concern for his horse drove everything else out of Jess's head, and he hobbled quickly to the door in his frozen boots, opened it, and confronted his visitor. It was not a ghost.

It was worse.

It was a wolf.

It sprang past him on to the heap of bedding still warm from Jess's sleeping.

'He won't hurt you!' called a voice. 'We stop here sometimes. I cook.'

It was his friend Sweet Rain. She came slowly towards him across the snowscape, her bright pinto pony picking its laborious way along the tracks left by the wolf. She wore a painted, blue flannel dress, a blanket around her head and body, and snowshoes were strapped across her back.

'It's a wolf!' squeaked Jess, peering in round the door.

'Only half. Didn't you know? We breed our dogs with wolves. It makes them strong.'

When Sweet Rain had tied up her pony, she looked around the hut with dismay. 'What have you done?' she asked, as if he must have wrecked the place on purpose.

He explained about the flue.

'You can't stay here. Come with me.'

'Where?'

'Home, of course. You have to leave Destiny here, or my cousins will take her. You ride up with me. Oh, and bring a dish.'

'But I have work to do!' Jess protested. 'I can't desert my post!'

'Your post deserted you, I think,' said Sweet

Rain, as three more turf sods fell out of the roof and shattered on the earth floor. 'Coming?'

They rode over seemingly trackless snow, Jess unable to recognise a single landmark. But the wolf-dog bounded confidently on ahead, and Sweet Rain followed it. There was no telling where the snow was shallow and where it was dangerously deep. If they strayed from the trail of pawprints, Jess and Sweet Rain and her pony might disappear up to their ears in snow.

'What were you doing?' he asked. 'Out by Number 5 cabin?'

'Looking for buffalo, of course,' she said. 'We all look for buffalo. There are so few.' She winced. 'None maybe.'

Jess swallowed hard. You did not need to know much to know that the tribes depended on the buffalo herds for food and fuel, shelter and tools. The herds were dwindling fast, thanks to the white man, and clearly no buffalo at all had yet appeared on the winter hunting grounds of the Lakota or Dakota Sioux. He trembled to think what scenes of squalor and suffering he was about to witness at Sweet Rain's encampment. How did they survive this kind of weather? wondered Jess: tent-dwellers with no stoves or sheepskin jackets or knitted underwear.

Then he saw the camp, pitched on a field of glistening snow. It formed a letter C, its opening to the east. Smoke rose from every smoke flap, where the dozen or so decorated poles emerged from within the vast cone-shape tipis. The multitude of colours – the spots and stripes and animal drawings on the tents – along with the silver of a stream nearby, took his breath away.

The closer they got, the more nervous Sweet Rain became about bringing her 'outsider' friend home. 'Remember, don't call us Sioux. I know you think that's our name, but it isn't. We are the Lakota. Only our enemies call us Sioux.'

'Lakota. Lakota,' said Jess, practising. 'I never knew that before. I'm sorry if I insulted you – you know – before.'

Sweet Rain was reminded why she liked Jess so much. He had such good manners. They entered the encampment and rode up to the finest tent of all, the Chief's tent. 'We may go in. The door is open,' she said, with some relief.

'You go in from the right, me from the left. Don't walk between the fire and the Chief. Don't talk unless he speaks to you. And if he scrapes out his pipe, we must all get up and leave.'

'Right. Fire. Keep quiet. Pipe,' said Jess, trying to remember. Then he ducked inside through the oval doorway, and the warmth and the sights he saw put it all out of his head.

The inside of the tent seemed enormous, like the spire of a church but warmer. There was no eye-stinging fug of smoke, no clammy dampness. Drums and headdresses, quivers and breast plates swung from the roof, each brightly decorated, while eight exquisite dew-clothes lined the hide walls, soaking up the condensation from the cooking. A woman was frying pancakes. She looked up and stared in such alarm that Jess fixed his eyes shyly on the pancake in the pan, watching it slowly bubble and burn. After a long silence, Chief Golden Eagle addressed a few words to Sweet Rain, allowing her to speak.

'This is my friend, Jess Ford,' said Sweet Rain. (He could work out that much.) 'His house fell down.'

There was much laughter as Sweet Rain described the fate of Number 5. Jess nervously joined in, while his eyes travelled on round the beautiful conical room full of treasured and sacred objects. They travelled up to where, stretched on a wooden frame, a cured cow hide had been hung to tan in the smoke from the fire.

There was a big Lazy J brand scorched on it.

When he lowered his eyes, he was looking directly into the gaze of Chief Golden Eagle.

Quite a lot depended on what he said next: Jess could tell that from the spellbinding silence in the tent. They knew that he knew that they had killed and eaten a Lazy J steer. The veins were swollen in the Chief's temples, and his lips were pursed with embarrassment.

'May I speak?' Jess asked Sweet Rain. She bit her lip and nodded. 'Please tell Chief Golden Eagle I am pleased that the Lakota people accepted my bossman's gift of a cow, in this their time of hunger.'

Sweet Rain translated. The Chief breathed out and nodded. The dreadful moment was past.

A young child, pinch-faced and slightly potbellied with hunger, tottered up to Jess, so he started tossing a silver dollar to make the child laugh. The mother liked that. She asked if Jess had brought his eating bowl. And soon Jess was sharing their frugal meal of pancakes. (He was not even given the burnt one!)

In a basket near the door, a litter of sleeping puppies woke up and tumbled over each other. Jess forgot all his protocol. 'Are they yours, Sweet Rain? From your wolf?'

'No. They belong to the Chief.'

He rushed across the tent to scoop up the prettiest. 'Gee! Aren't they the best-looking puppies ever?' His foot upset a bowl of meal as he trampled right between the fire and Golden Eagle. Sweet Rain covered her face with her hands.

But before Jess could apologise, a shout went up outside which brought everyone to their feet. Buffalo!

Suddenly they were all running. The men were snatching up their weapons and snow-shoes, the women were restraining boys too young to hunt, the shamans were chanting, and brandishing magic charms.

'Oh please, God, let there be buffalo,' Jess found himself saying.

He told Sweet Rain she must not go – it was too dangerous – but of course she took no notice. Besides, he wanted to ride on her horse, be there, see a buffalo hunted as they had been hunted for centuries by men armed only with bows and spears.

A small group of buffalo had been sighted in difficult, uneven terrain. The hunters had to abandon their horses and go on foot. And they all had snowshoes, whereas Jess had none.

He struggled and floundered after them, sinking to the knee at each step. How could men on foot hunt down a bison anyway? 'We'll drive it into a snowdrift!' Sweet Rain called back over her shoulder as she too strode out across the printless snow on her willow-weave paddle-shaped shoes.

Suddenly four beasts as big and black as locomotives were in among the hunters, found almost by accident and set running. The animals did not run away; they simply ran, kicking up a blizzard of snow as they went. One hunter was knocked down by the lead bison and trampled by a second. Spears flew, but the creatures were moving too fast, and the huntsmen too slow on foot.

Infuriatingly, there was no knowing where the snow was deep and where it was shallow – no obvious curving drifts. The hunters might manage to drive the bison, but in which direction should they be driven?

It was taking all Jess's energy just to keep his feet when, all of a sudden, the black shaggy monsters turned and came charging back towards him. He jumped – hurled himself head-over-heels as far as he could possibly leap – and sank up to his waist in deep snow, while the buffalo galloped on by, churning the whiteness to a slush.

It was not cold; Jess simply could not move. When he tried to climb out, he sank even farther, up to his chest. What if a bison came his way now, trampling his head like some fircone on a forest path? He wriggled some more and only sank up to his neck. It was all he could do to keep his upraised hands free of the snow.

But of course! If a bison came his way then it, too, would be trapped! It too would wallow and sink in the soft powdery quicksand snow. 'This way, you brutes!' hollered Jess. 'Come this way!' He lost sight of the danger. He could only think of that single, desperate need – to trap the first buffalo of winter. 'Come this way, why don't you!'

Incensed by the prick of arrows and the shrieks of the hunters, the bison wheeled once more and careered over the same slushy ground. The Lakota men began to tire and drop, unable to run another step in their snowshoes, unable to keep up. Sweet Rain saw Jess mired in the deep snow. She tried to tell the others of the danger he was in. But there was nothing they could do to reach him ahead of the four bison.

'Come and get me!' chanted Jess, as if baiting a schoolyard bully. Three of the stampeding bison ignored him, refusing to be deflected from their manic gallop. But the fourth saw the wag of Jess's arms, heard him shout, and excited, like a bull in a bull-ring, ducked its enormous head and veered towards him.

That buffalo seemed to fill Jess's vision, seemed to hurtle down on him, a black meteorite out of a white sky. But as the bison's thrashing legs sank into the soft snow, it pitched forward, lost its balance, rolled and fell. Its enormous bulk carried it along, skidding and sinking, nose down, tail up. It finally came to rest with its stinking beard warming Jess's face, melting the snow in his hair.

The women were already dancing when the hunting party got back. Though the prize had still to be dragged home, the news had reached every woman and child and old person: the first buffalo of winter had been killed. It alone might last them through till springtime. Not one hair, not one hoof would go to waste.

Jess was singing, Sweet Rain was singing, even the man who had been trampled was singing, as his friends dragged him home on a makeshift sled pulled by a horse. They none of them even felt the gnawing cold.

Then Jess spotted two Lazy J strays pawing miserably at the snow, uncovering grass to eat. He stopped singing. He knew he ought to be driving them homewards. That was what he got paid for. As Obadiah Thorn would have said: 'You're a cowboy, son, not an injun.'

'I must get back to Number 5,' he said to Sweet Rain. 'Will you take me, please?'

'Chief Golden Eagle wants you.'

'Me? Why? What have I done? Was it my bad manners?'

Sweet Rain only shrugged.

The doorflap of the tipi was raised, permitting entry. Jess ducked inside. 'Keep right, not between the fire . . . keep quiet . . . pipe,' he reminded himself. But this time what he noticed were the tomahawks and meat knives hanging from the roof, the red spotted feather in the Chief's hair which meant he had killed a man in battle.

Even after the success of the hunt the Chief was still not smiling; he was far too important for smiling. His weatherbeaten face was a whorl of wrinkles as he held out something towards Jess. 'For Jessford,' he said.

It was one of the puppies.

After three weeks of chilly solitude, Woolly rode up from Number 3 to Number 4 cabin and collected Jingle Bobs. They rode up to Number 6 and collected Obadiah Thorn. Together the three went to Number 5, planning to stay the night with Jess before heading back for their cosy bunkhouse at the Lazy J. Jess was outdoors chopping wood in the twilight when they arrived. Number 5 was fixed up as good as new.

'Lonely enough for you, was it, boy?' said Obadiah, knowing how three weeks of line camp usually felt like three years.

'Oooh, I wouldn't say lonely. Plenty work to do. Home cooking. Good company,' said Jess.

The cowhands looked at one another, confused. 'Company?'

'Well, the ghost, of course. Can't you hear him? What's the matter? He's okay when you get to know him.'

Sure enough, an unearthly whimpering howl was coming from the hut. Obadiah, Woolly and Jingle Bobs all turned as white as the snow. Obadiah was first to recover himself. He strode boldly up to the cabin. 'Nah. The boy's joking. Aren't you, boy? You're joking, aren't you?' His hand grasped the latch, but he did not lift it.

'Sure I'm joking,' said Jess, setting down his axe, pushing his hat back off his face, grinning.

Obadiah laughed with relief.

'Not a ghost at all,' said Jess.

Obadiah lifted the latch.

'It's a wolf.'

7

Dandy Dude

He called his dog Ghost, and a prettier dog you never saw unless you saw one half dog, half wolf. Jess fed him and groomed him, made him up a bed in the bunkhouse, and taught him not to go fouling up indoors, when there was a million acres more suitable outside. Ghost and Destiny got along just fine, and the other cowhands got used, after a while, to having a half-wolf sleeping in with them.

But Bossman J said, 'No. Git that critter out of my bunkhouse and off this ranch. Cows scare easy. If they see a wolf, they're gonna run their hoofs off. So listen up, Jess Ford. If you want to go on working at the Lazy J, you get rid of that hound!'

Poor Jess. He was pretty fond of that dog, and he seriously considered leaving, then and there. But first and foremost Jess was a cowboy, and if he went to another ranch the rules would probably be the same: no dogs. So Jess put his puppy over his saddle bow and went into town. He figured maybe his friend Doctor Luke might take in Ghost and give him a good home.

'Sorry,' said the doctor. 'I have to keep my consulting rooms spotless, and dogs don't understand about spotless.'

Sheriff Sparrow said much the same. 'Cain't keep a dog, son. It's in the rule books. "Specially not wolf-dogs," it says.'

That settled it. Jess would have to leave the Lazy J, and go on the road with his dog. If only he had more money saved up!

As he walked down the main street, his puppy at his heels and his heart in his boots, he saw a stranger come out of the bank. Jess had never seen anyone like this before. The stranger wore a yellow plaid jacket, loud as a brass band, and thin, shiny, black trousers with a band of satin down each leg. Lace cuffs frothed out below his velvet cuffs, and a white lace cravat spilled over his velvet collar, fastened with a gold pin. His hat had a crown so low it made his head look flat on top, and his boots had heels so high that he walked on tiptoe.

'Say, boy! That's a fine puppy dog you got there!' said the stranger to Jess. 'I'll play you for him!'

'Play me?'

'Cards. Poker. You do play cards, I suppose.'

Gambling was forbidden at the Lazy J. But the girls at the Silver Dollar had once taught Jess rummy, and he knew snap, too, and solitaire. 'Sure,' he said.

Half an hour later, Jess came out of the Comfort Hotel with no dog at his heels and a feeling in his heart he had been robbed.

When he told his workmates about losing his dog in a poker game, they were livid. 'Play a boy for his dog? Who is this son of a corn-stealing crow?'

'His name's Dandy Dude,' said Jess miserably. 'Leastways that's what he gets called.'

'Well, I'll ruffle his lace for him 'fore he's a day older!' Obadiah vowed, and away he went to town, with Jingle Bobs and Woolly tagging along. Bossman J (though glad to be rid of the wolf-dog off his ranch) said, 'Wouldn't have won at poker against *me*. No, sir! No one beats me at poker.'

Obadiah played Dandy Duke at poker, to

win back Jess's dog. But all that happened was that he lost his silver pocket watch, the one his grandpa left him.

Then Woolly played Dandy Duke at poker, to win back Jess's dog and Obadiah's pocket watch. But all that happened was that Woolly lost his magnificent curly goatskin chaps or overtrousers, the ones that gave him his nickname.

After that, Jingle Bobs played Dandy Dude, to win back Jess's dog and Obadiah's pocket watch and Woolly's goatskin chaps. But all that happened was that Jingle Bobs lost his fancy spurs with the star-pinwheels on the back, the ones that had given him *his* nickname.

When Bossman J heard about it, he tut-tutted for an hour and said three times over, 'He wouldn't have beaten me at poker, this Dandy Dude. No one ever does.'

The four friends sat about, miserable as a treeful of wet leaves, and bemoaned their losses. 'We're not the only ones, that's some comfort. He sits there, that corn dolly, in his yellow tartan jacket . . .'

'It's purple in the morning. Purple jacket in the morning, yellow in the afternoon.'

'. . . luring the people in to play him.'

'Like a spider trapping flies,' Jingle agreed.

'Like a mermaid wrecking sailors,' said Woolly poetically.

Suddenly, there was a scratching noise at the barn door, and in squeezed Ghost, covered in white dust from the road, his tongue hanging out for a drink.

'You came home to me!' cried Jess, hugging his dog close.

'Wish my pocket watch had legs,' saaid Obadiah gloomily, 'and could fetch itself home where it belongs.'

But next morning, Dandy Dude turned up at the Lazy J, driving a surrey. He had come looking for Ghost. 'No one loses a thing to me and takes it back,' he said without removing the black cigar from the corner of his mouth.

'I didn't take him back, honest! He found his own way!'

'Same difference. No one loses a thing to me and gets to keep it.'

'Maybe he didn't like being in town,' said Jess, as polite as possible.

'Well, unless you like being in jail,' snarled Dandy Dude, 'you just tie that dog on behind, and count yourself lucky I didn't set the Sheriff on you. If it happens again, I will!'

Jess felt as if he had lost his dog twice over, but there was nothing to be done. Even Bossman J was vexed by the man's bullying manner and flashy ways, but he could not intervene: a gambling debt is a gambling debt. He confined himself to muttering: 'Playing poker with a boy his age! You wouldn't have won so easy against a *real* poker player.'

'Is that a challenge, rancher?' said Dandy Dude, quick as lightning. 'Nothing I enjoy better than playing poker with an expert. So long as the stakes are high enough. See you in the Comfort Hotel tomorrow. High noon.'

Now Bossman J's wife was dead against gambling, and Bossman had not actually been allowed to play a hand of cards since his wedding day. But he was not about to admit that. So he just raised his hat, wiped his brow and said, 'Mebbe. We'll see.'

Away went Dandy Dude, Ghost tied behind the buggy, stretching his poor little neck to keep up. Watching, Jess thought, That's the last I'll see of you, little Ghost.

Then, very early next morning, he was

woken by a warm weight on his feet, and there, stretched out across the quilt, was Ghost. He had made up his mind not to belong to Dandy Dude but to go where he was loved.

'Oh Ghost, Ghost! You've really done for me, now! That gambling man will set the law on me this time, for sure!' He pulled the dog on to his lap and sat scratching and stroking it and tugging fondly at its wolfish ears, while it licked his hands. 'It's no good, Ghost. I've got to get you back to Dandy Dude before he has me thrown in jail. And you have to stay with him, like it or not. He won you fair and square . . . and I guess you'll grow to like him, one fine day.'

Jess carried his clothes and boots outside and dressed in the yard, so as not to disturb the other men. He was just going into the tack room for Destiny's saddle when he bumped into Bossman J coming out, dressed in his Sunday suit.

'I'm sorry, sir. Ghost came back again,' said Jess nervously. 'I figured I'd take him straight back into town, if you can spare me. You heard what Dandy Dude said he'd do.'

'I'll keep you company on the ride, son. I was just going in to town myself.'

They rode in silence for a long while before Jess plucked up the courage to ask, 'You're not going to play poker with that dude, are you, sir?'

Bossman J flushed a deep crimson. 'I may look in at the hotel around lunchtime. Play a couple of hands. Teach the man a lesson.' Then he rounded on Jess, jabbing an angry finger in the boy's face. 'But don't you go telling Mrs J, you hear?'

'Not a word, boss!' Jess promised. But in view of the lost pocket watch, the chaps, the spurs, the dog, he thought Mrs J might be right when she said gambling was 'the cleverest piece of foolishness the devil ever invented'.

They were friends again by the time they reached town. 'I'll keep the dude busy with a quick game, while you sneak that dog back into his room,' Bossman suggested.

'Would you do that, sir? Would you?'

'I will, if you be sure to tie him up tight to the bedpost, so he can't git loose again!'

The hotel manager did not allow dogs upstairs – 'especially not wolves!' he said – so

Jess had to go round to the outside stairs at the back of the hotel, and sneak like a burglar up to the first floor. He was in luck. The first window he looked in at, he could see cards on the bed and the yellow tartan jacket hung over the back of the chair. The room was empty. Dandy Dude must be downstairs in the bar, wearing his purple plaid jacket, playing Bossman J at poker. Jess slid the window up and climbed in.

The dog in his arms began to whimper, associating the smell of the room with the man he so detested. But Jess took no notice. So what if his eyes were full of tears as he knotted Ghost's lead to the pedpost? So what if the little fellow strained after him with every fibre of his wolf-grey body as he went to climb back out of the window. Dandy Dude had won Ghost fair and square, and a gambling debt must be honoured.

Suddenly Jess blinked the tears out of his eyes and looked again. There was something odd about the way that jacket was spread out so very carefully over the chair. Jess took a closer look. The lining seemed to have several extra rows of very fine stitching; the corner of a playing card was just showing above the black velvet cuff of the left sleeve.

Once Jess really started looking, he found sixteen aces and colour cards hidden in the various secret compartments of that most unusual jacket. 'Mighty fine piece of tailoring, Mister Dandy Dude,' said Jess under his breath. 'One run of luck guaranteed all morning, then you come back here, change your jacket, and you're ready for another winning streak in the afternoon. You, sir, are a cheat and a card-sharper, and today, sir, is the day your luck runs out!' Fetching the spare cards from the bed, Jess set about making one or two adjustments to Dandy Dude's yellow tartan jacket. Then, untying his dog, they both left the way they had come, through the window.

By the time Jess and Ghost arrived in the hotel bar, Bossman J was sweating like a racehorse. He sat hunched over a hand of playing cards, his face screwed into a grimace of despair. Neighbours, stockmen, cowboys and townsfolk stood around shaking their heads. Bossman J was already up to his neck in debt, and betting larger and larger sums in an effort to win back his money.

'I just think I've got him licked and he lays down a pair of aces!' he hissed at Jess. 'The man's got the luck of the devil!'

'Not for long he hasn't,' whispered Jess in return. 'Trust me.'

Across the table, Dandy Dude looked up and saw Jess, his fingers through the collar of the wolf-dog. 'That's *my* dog you've got there, boy,' he said sourly.

'Just exercising him for you, sir,' said Jess. 'He got loose but I caught him for you. Shall I take him back to your room?'

'What? Oh. No. I'll put him back myself. Time for a change of clothes, anyway. I do like to stay neat while I play.'

Bossman J, hands trembling, eyes bulging with misery, chewed on his pocket handkerchief and totted up his losses. 'I'm ruined, Jess! What's Mrs J gonna say? I must be plum loco!'

Dandy Dude came back and sat down opposite, wearing yellow.

'You'll win it back, sir. I know you will.'

'But you don't understand, boy! I've got nothing left to bet with. Nothing!'

'You've got the ranch, sir. Bet the Lazy J.'

Dandy Dude champed delightedly on his

cigar. 'Now there's a boy who knows how to gamble with style! What d'you say, rancher? Will you bet me your spread against everything you've lost this morning?'

The spectators groaned with horror. Bossman J – such a popular man, such a respected citizen of Sundown – was about to lose the Lazy J to a worthless gambler. They could hardly bear to watch.

'No! I won't do it,' said Bossman J. 'It's all I got!'

'Yes,' said Jess Ford. 'He will. Now deal, Dandy Dude!'

And do you know what? The next time Dandy Dude flourished his cards, and laid them down on the table saying, 'I win!' his was not a winning hand at all, only two 2s, a 3 and a 5. And when he cried, 'A pair of aces!' it was only a worthless 5 and a grinning joker. 'I – I don't understand! I –' stammered the gambler, his eyes on stalks.

'Deal!' said Bossman J, and the game went on till he had won back Obadiah's pocket watch, Woolly's chaps and Jingle's spurs. You never saw so many worthless hands as Dandy Dude drew that afternoon, and with every one he grew a little more wild-eyed, a little hotter under his white lace collar.

In the end he made an excuse to go to his room. 'For more money to bet!' he said.

'Fine. So long as you leave your jacket here,' said Jess.

That was when Dandy Dude knew he had been found out for a cheat. He knew, too, who had switched all the aces and colour cards hidden in his jacket for worthless, low-value cards.

He slid out of the jacket and ran for the stairs, thinking to grab his bags and flee down the back staircase. Meanwhile, Jess gathered everybody around to demonstrate to them the interesting features of Dandy Dude's loud yellow jacket. When they saw just how the gambler had cheated them, the whole town took off up the hotel stairs, howling for vengeance.

There was really no need.

As he opened his bedroom door, Dandy was met by a flying thunderbolt of grey fur. Ghost, making one last bid for freedom, knocked him backwards, so that he tripped on the top stairs and came tumbling down the hotel stairs all mixed up with paws and fur and a wolfish tail.

The townsfolk of Sundown saw to it that Dandy Dude left a lesser man than he had come. They took back every red cent he had won from them (and a bit more, to pay for a new church gate). Then they tied him on to his horse backwards, and rode him out of town.

All this while, Bossman J stayed put in the hotel. His knees were too shaky to carry him. He had come terribly close to ruin that day, and he needed time to recover. Jess fetched him a drink of soothing milk, as well as a bowl of water for Ghost, then pulled up a chair and sank his face on his fists.

'Know anyone who needs a dog, boss? Half dog, half wolf?'

Bosman J drank his milk. 'Reckon I do, boy.'

'Who's that? Gotta take good care of him, mind!'

'Oh, I reckon he'd do that, the man I'm thinking of. He's good with animals.'

Jess brightened a little. 'Who? Is he local? I'll take Ghost there now.'

Bossman J licked the white circle of milk

from around his mouth, like a cheerful cat, and grinned. 'I'll ride along with you. After all, he works out at my place. Name of Jess Ford. Just ask for Cowboy Jess.'